Bedwetting, Dry Nights

Bedtime Healing Meditation for Children

Little Blue Zen

Bedwetting, Dry Nights

Copyright@ 2024 Jo Galloway

The right of the author has been asserted to her following the copyright writing, designs and patent act of Australia.

All rights reserved. No part of this book may be reproduced, stored or transmitted by any means whether auditory, graphic, mechanical, or electronic without the written permission of the author. Unauthorised reproduction of any part of this work is illegal and is punishable by law.

Unless otherwise noted, the author and the publisher make no explicit guarantees as the accuracy of the information contained in this book may differ based on individual experiences and context

ISBN: 978-1-7635801-5-2

Published by Little Blue Zen
Birdwood NSW
Printed in Australia
Cover Design: Gagan Karunachandra
Editing: Kristine Gibson
jo@littlebluezen.com
http://www.littlebluezen.com

Bedwetting, Dry Nights

Bedtime Healing Meditation for Children

Jo Galloway

Your child may like other books in this series

- Bully Proof. Keeping out the bullies.

- I am Different, I am Me.

- The Magical Treasure Hunt. Building Confidence.

- The Magical Worry Balloon.

- Angelic Dreams. Meet your Guardian Angel.

- Scared of the Dark.

- I Love School.

- A Coat of Flying Colours

INTRODUCTION

Why Healing Meditations.

As children we make sense of our experiences based on our limited understanding and perception. We may misinterpret events or draw conclusions that form the basis of limiting beliefs that influence our entire life. These beliefs become ingrained over time, shaping our thoughts, feelings and behaviours well into adulthood unless consciously challenged.

In my work as a practising Hypnotherapist, I've found that all my clients' concerns, whether rooted in fears, feelings of inadequacy, addictive behaviours, or other challenges, trace back to their early childhood experiences, interactions, and upbringing. It's important to note that these issues don't exclusively stem from abusive or dysfunctional environments; limiting beliefs can arise from various circumstances.

Parents or caregivers wield substantial influence in shaping our perceptions of ourselves and the world around us. Remarks, criticisms, or comparisons made by family members can foster beliefs about our capabilities, worthiness, or potential. Furthermore, interactions with peers, teachers, and authority figures also contribute to the formation of these beliefs. Repeated experiences of rejection or failure can solidify beliefs such as "I'm not good enough" or "I'm unworthy of love."

This realzsation ignited my passion for intervening at the source: working with children to prevent these beliefs from taking root and manifesting into significant challenges in adulthood. By addressing issues early on, we can guide children to develop into the best versions of themselves, free from the burden of limiting beliefs that could otherwise dominate their lives.

.

2 * DRY NIGHTS

How Healing Meditation will help your child.

Teaching children meditation offers a multitude of benefits that can positively influence their daily lives and overall development. A regular mindfulness meditation practice provides valuable tools for managing stress, navigating emotions, and promoting overall well-being. Healing meditations, in particular, bolster your child's self-belief, helping to remove any resistance they may face in adulthood. This leads to a happier, more successful and fulfilling life.

Unlike traditional meditation, which often centres on relaxation, healing meditations go a step further by focusing on recovery, balance, and reprogramming a child's self-belief. These meditations use techniques such as breathing exercises, visualization, and guided imagery to not only foster deep relaxation but also reshape their mindset.

This targeted approach helps build a stronger sense of self-confidence and resilience. By integrating positive affirmations and emotional healing, healing meditations offer a distinct advantage over traditional methods, laying a powerful foundation for a child's future success and well-being.

Meditation can also be an effective part of your child's bedtime routine, helping to calm the mind and prepare the body for restful sleep. Techniques like guided imagery and deep breathing, as outlined in this book, can signal to the brain that it's time to wind down.

Sharing these calming moments at bedtime not only strengthens the bond between parent and child, but also creates a supportive and nurturing environment. It also sets a positive example, emphasizing the importance of self-care and mindfulness.

With patience and consistency, you can help your child develop a lifelong practice that supports their mental, emotional, and physical health. Give your child the gift of relaxation and imagination with this easy-to-read story designed to inspire and uplift.

Bedwetting, Dry Nights

DRY NIGHTS is a soothing bedtime meditation designed to help children aged 3 to 7 wake up to a dry bed each morning. This gentle and magical story, uses comforting language and imagery to empower young listeners to reconnect their brain and bladder, fostering better control and confidence throughout the night.

The story begins with a calming "Sleeping Meditation" preparing your child to absorb the positive suggestions woven throughout the story. Through engaging dialogue and vivid imagery children are guided to relax deeply, feel secure, and visualize their bladder and brain working together in harmony.

The meditation encourages children to focus on their breath and sensations, helping them understand their body's signals. It emphasizes the powerful connection between their special brain and their bladder, teaching them to recognize when they need to wake up and use the toilet.

As children drift off to sleep, they are gently reminded of their newfound ability to stay dry all night, no matter where they sleep. The story ends with a comforting affirmation of their success and control, ensuring that each night is a step towards waking up happy and dry.

Perfect for bedtime routines, **DRY NIGHTS** helps children build confidence, establish positive habits, and embrace their inner strength for a restful, dry night's sleep. With repeated listening, this story reinforces positive messages and builds a sense of control and empowerment.

DRY NIGHTS, is also available on YouTube, providing a soothing auditory experience children can enjoy at home, in the car, or anywhere they need a moment of relaxation.

Listen on YouTube

Bedwetting, Dry Nights

Hello, my little Starlight.

A little birdie told me you've had a few accidents at night, but don't worry! Tonight, we're going to do something very special and magical.

Soon you will wake up nice and dry every morning.

Won't that be cool?

No matter where you sleep, whether it's at a friend's house, at camp, or on a school trip. You won't have to worry about wet sheets anymore.

And guess what?
Mummy and Daddy will be so happy!
What a great feeling that will be to wake up dry every morning.
Do you know what this magic is called?
It is called Sleeping Meditation.
Sleeping Meditation is a special kind of rest where you're asleep, but not asleep.
You're awake, but not fully awake either.
This magical rest helps you learn new things, feel calm, happy and ready to do anything.
Did you know children have a very special brain?

But your special brain has not been talking to your bladder.

Do you know what a bladder is?

Your bladder is a little bag inside your tummy that holds all your wee.

Sometimes, your bladder forgets to tell your special brain when it's full, so you might not wake up in time to go to the toilet.

But don't worry, we're going to fix that- easy peasy.

Are you ready to get started?

Are you ready for some magic?

Have a little wiggle and find your perfect spot.

Make yourself comfy and snuggle up.
Pull your blankets up so you're warm and cozy.
Take a big, long stretch—stretch your body out.
Oh, that feels so nice, doesn't it?
Now uncross your legs and place your hands gently by your sides.
Make sure you're nice and comfortable.
Now let's take a big, deep breath in...
and breathe out, as if you were blowing out all your birthday candles.
Phewww.....
Perfect!

Let's do that again, shall we?

Take a big breath in…like you're smelling a beautiful flower.

This time, as you breathe out, blowing out your candles, softly close your eyelids down, all the way down.

As your eyelids close, you're beginning to feel sleepier and sleepier.

Breathing in and out, in and out, as your belly rises and falls.

Wonderful!

Feel your body become all loose and floppy.

Loose and floppy, like a jellyfish.

You're beginning to feel heavier and heavier as you sink down into your beautiful, soft, warm bed.

Your eyes are so very heavy and tied.

Your head is gently sinking into the pillow.

Your cozy bed holds you in a big, wonderful cuddle as your body relaxes like a puppet.

You feel so warm and safe.

Ahh, your bed feels amazing tonight.

As you sink down, drift down, you begin to feel so sleepy.

Sleepy is moving down your body, across your shoulders and down your arms.

Sleepy is flowing down your back, sliding down your legs, through your feet and even into your toes.

Feel your toes begin to tingle.

Did you know children have a very special brain?

A special brain that tells your heart to beat and your hair to grow all by itself.

You're so clever, you definitely have a special brain!

Your special brain is like a superhero. It helps you think, dream, and imagine amazing things.

It makes sure you can run, play, and even learn new things every day

Now, my little Starlight, put all your attention on your tummy as it rises up and falls down with every breath you take.

Breathe in, tummy rises up and breathe out, tummy goes down, up and down.

With your special brain, I what you to look inside your tummy as it rises and falls and find your bladder.

Your bladder is the balloon that holds all your wee.

Can you picture what colour it might be?

Your special brain is always awake and looking after you, even when you're fast asleep.

Your special brain helps you breathe in the air around you and keeps your heart pumping, all without you ever having to tell it.

It keeps you safe and even helps grow your fingernails.

When your bladder sends a message saying, "I am full," your special brain will send a little signal to wake you up so you can go to the toilet and do a wee.

Tonight, while you're fast asleep and dreaming the most amazing and adventurous dreams, your special brain will keep looking after you.

When your bladder becomes full, it sends a powerful message to your special brain, telling you to wake up and go to the toilet.

Your special brain will wake you up and you'll know it is time to get up and go to the toilet and wee.

You'll see the magic happen all be itself.

You've taught your bladder to send a message to your special brain when it's full.

Your special brain will wake up and you'll get out of bed and go to the toilet and do a wee.

Your bladder is doing a great job!

But lately, your bladder has forgotten to wake up your special brain.

Silly bladder!

But now it remembers when it feels full, and before it gets too full, it will send a strong message to your brilliant, special brain, saying, "WAKE UP!"

Then you'll get up and go to the toilet to wee.

You've discovered a new superpower within you!

A new way to control your body with your special brain makes you feel amazing and back in control.

You feel thrilled, delighted and excited.

Woo hoo - dry nights, here you come!

With your super brilliant, special brain, you can do anything.

You can stay dry all night, every night, no matter where you sleep.

You wake up dry and proud of yourself every day because you are amazing, and your special brain is incredible.

Your super amazing, clever brain will do this every single night from now on and for the rest of your life.

You are so happy because YOU ARE BACK IN CONTROL!

With the power of your special brain, you can do anything you want in your life.

Each and every night, you stay TOTALLY DRY, and that makes you so happy.

You're doing an amazing job, Little Starlight.

Well done!

The past is behind you.

Your special brain and your bladder are back on track working together to help you stay nice and dry all night long.

You're growing more confident each and every night.

You love bedtimes now.

Old worries are gone for good.

Your bladder is back in the game.

Now you only ever use the toilet to wee, never the bed, because you do things in the right way, at the right time, and in the right place.

Well done!

Imagine your bladder now, looking calm, relaxed, and happy.

Your bladder loves its job of keeping you dry.

Picture yourself waking up each morning completely dry.

You feel so happy to be dry every single day.

20 * DRY NIGHTS

You're excited and thrilled with yourself!

You feel amazing now that your special brain and bladder are back on the job of keeping you dry.

You now wake up each and every time your bladder is full.

When your special brain gets the message from your full bladder, you hop out of bed, walk to the toilet and do a wee.

You quickly feel sleepy again, hop back into bed and before you know it you're fast asleep as soon as your special brain hits the pillow.

Dry nights every night -Woo hoo!

When you wake up in the morning, your bed is dry, your pjs are dry and you feel warm, dry and happy.

You feel so good because you are back in charge, back in control.

You are the captain of your ship and have taken full charge of your bladder.

You're so excited when you wake up you jump out of bed and race to tell everyone.

They'll see the big smile on your face!

You tell them my bed is dry and you do a little happy dance.

Everyone is so proud of you.

Well done, Little Starlight!

Let yourself become sleepier now.

You love the power of being in control of your bladder and feeling so good about yourself.

You know that when your bladder becomes full, it will send a powerful message to your genius special brain to WAKEUP.

With unshakable confidence, you know you will wake up, get up and automatically go to the toilet for a wee, every time night or day.

Your special brain will never let you down.

So now it is time to drift off to sleep and dream the most magical dreams.

Rest easy, knowing your bladder is back on track and you have complete control.

You'll wake up in the morning to a wonderful dry bed.

Well done, Little Starlight.

Sweet Dreams.

Also by Jo Galloway

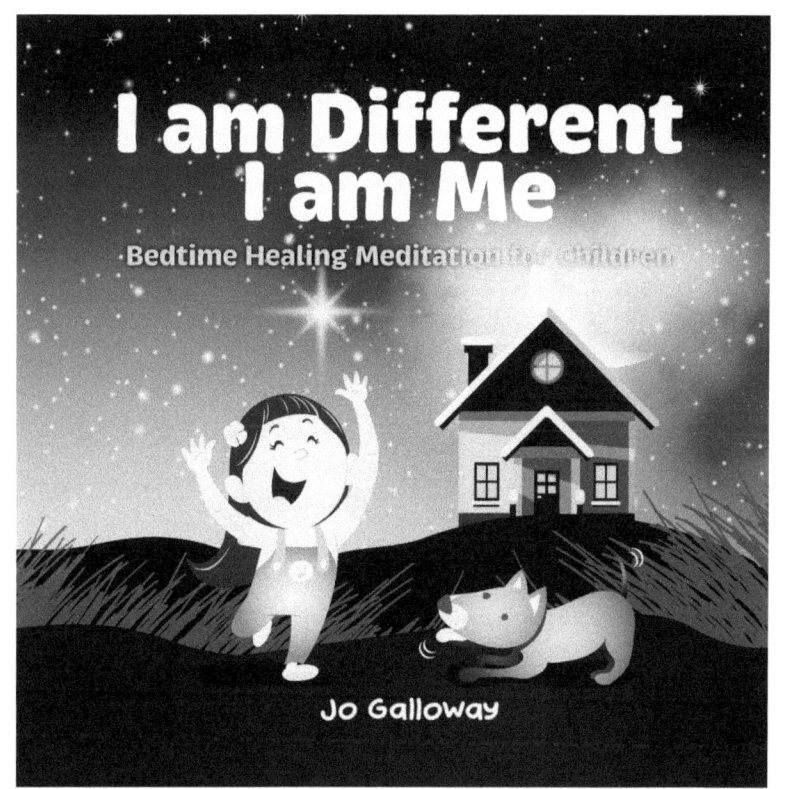

In a world where everyone is unique and special, being different is something to celebrate! "I Am Different, I Am Me" is a delightful bedtime story that shows just how wonderful it is to be yourself.

It's all about embracing our differences, celebrating our uniqueness, and feeling proud of who we are. This empowering meditation encourages your child to embrace their individuality and recognize their special gifts. They will discover the joy of being exactly who they were meant to be.

Give your child the gift of imagination and relaxation at bedtime with this easy-to-read story, designed to inspire and uplift.

Scared of the Dark

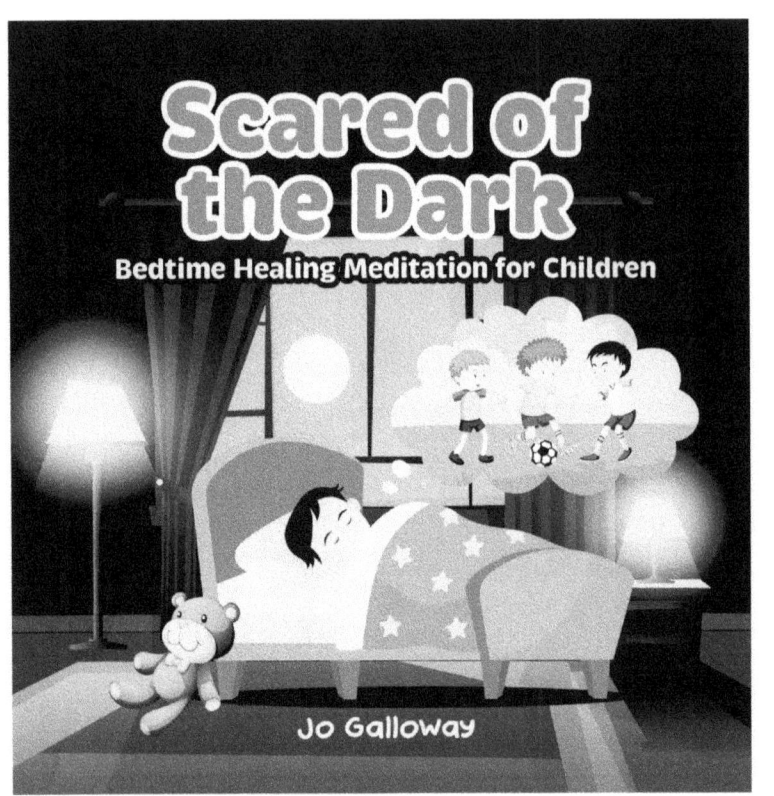

Join Teddy, your brave and comforting friend, on a magical bedtime journey designed to help little ones conquer their fears of the dark. In this gentle Healing Meditation, Teddy shares a heartwarming story about overcoming nighttime worries and using the power of your imagination to transform fear into bravery. Through soothing guidance, deep breathing and a comforting countdown, Teddy helps children relax deeply and embrace their inner courage. Ideal for easing bedtime anxieties, this meditation fosters a sense of safety and confidence, ensuring a peaceful, restful night's sleep.

Little Blue Zen.com

Little Blue Zen